Charlie

& The Tooth Fairy

Look out for other books in this series:

Charlie
& The Cat Flap

Charlie
& The Great Escape

Charlie
& The Big Snow

Charlie
& The Rocket Boy

Charlie
& The Cheese & Onion Crisps

Charlie
& The Haunted Tent

www.hilarymckay.co.uk

Charlie
& The Tooth Fairy

Hilary McKay

Illustrated by Sam Hearn

■SCHOLASTIC

To Thomas Cochrane
Thank you for all the good ideas!
From Hilary McKay

First published in the UK in 2009 by Scholastic Children's Books
An imprint of Scholastic Ltd
Euston House, 24 Eversholt Street
London, NW1 1DB, UK
Registered office: Westfield Road, Southam, Warwickshire, CV47 0RA
SCHOLASTIC and associated logos are trademarks and/or registered trademarks of
Scholastic Inc.

Text copyright © Hilary McKay, 2009
Illustrations copyright © Sam Hearn, 2009

The right of Hilary McKay and Sam Hearn to be identified as the author
and illustrator of this work has been asserted by them.

Cover illustration © Sam Hearn, 2009

ISBN 978 1 407 11088 2

A CIP catalogue record for this book is available
from the British Library

Printed by CPI Bookmarque, Croydon.
Papers used by Scholastic Children's Books are made from wood grown in
sustainable forests.

1 3 5 7 9 10 8 6 4 2

This is a work of fiction. Names, characters, places, incidents
and dialogues are products of the author's imagination or are used
fictitiously. Any resemblance to actual people, living or dead, events
or locales is entirely coincidental.

www.scholastic.co.uk/zone

ONE

The First Tooth

Charlie had four wobbly teeth.

He had:

One that was rather wobbly.

One that was quite
wobbly.

One that was slightly
wobbly.

One that was just

beginning to be wobbly.

He had them all together, and he was very excited about it because they were his first wobbly teeth.

Charlie also had a big brother called Max. Max was very clever. He knew things most other people didn't know, like what chewing gum was made of and how magnets worked and the way to tell if strange dogs were friendly or not. Max knew so much and was right so often that it was hardly worth arguing with him.

Whenever Charlie wanted to know something he would go to Max for the answer. And if he wanted to prove to anyone that something was true he would say, "If you don't believe me, ask Max!"

And then whoever Charlie was talking to would know that it really was true, because everyone knew how clever Max was.

So Max was a very useful brother to Charlie.

But Max was not useful when Charlie discovered that he had four wobbly teeth.

Charlie showed Max his wobbliest tooth, and asked, "How can I make it come out faster?"

Max looked at the tooth and said, "You can't. It's not that loose! It might be there for ages yet! Anyway, what's the hurry?"

"I need it for the tooth fairy," said
Charlie, with his fingers in his mouth,
giving his wobbliest tooth an extra wobble.
Charlie was very much looking forward
to getting his teeth out, one by one, and
leaving them under his pillow for the tooth
fairy. His best friend, Henry, had told him
about her.

"The tooth fairy!" repeated Max. "The
tooth fairy is for kids!"

"For kids?"

"Yes, *and*," said Max, "the tooth fairy is
a waste of teeth!"

"*A waste of teeth*?"

"You'll find out!" said Max, walking
away.

After Max had gone, Charlie remembered
that his brother had always been like this

about the tooth fairy. When Max's own teeth had fallen out he had not put them under his pillow. He had hidden them away in a secret place instead.

"Who wants fairies crawling around their bed while they're asleep?" Max had asked. "And what kind of person sells *their own teeth*?"

Max was no help at all about wobbly teeth, but Charlie's best friend, Henry, was.

Henry was an expert on teeth. Four of his had come out already. He didn't care. He liked the gaps. He had pulled all four out himself, and enjoyed doing it.

He thought he might be a dentist one day, just for the pleasure of pulling out teeth.

When Charlie's wobbliest tooth refused to get any more wobbly and it began to look like it really wouldn't be out for ages (just like Max had said), Henry kindly offered to help speed it up.

"If you're really sure you want it out," he said.

"Of course I am!"

"Well then," said Henry. "You need a method. In fact, you need *The Newly Invented Look At The Lovely View Method*."

"Do I?"

"Trust me, I'm an expert," said Henry, and Charlie, who knew that in the matter of teeth Henry really was an expert, said, "OK."

Then Henry went home and returned

with a reel of dental floss.

"We need to go up to your bedroom," he told Charlie.

"Why?"

"So you can look at the lovely view," said Henry.

Upstairs in Charlie's bedroom, Henry tied a long piece of dental floss to Charlie's tooth.

Then he looked around for something heavy to tie on the other end.

"A rock would be good," said Henry.

Unfortunately Charlie did not have any rocks in his bedroom, but he did have a quite heavy *Doctor Who* TARDIS.

"It'll have to do," said Henry, and made the TARDIS very much heavier by stuffing inside three Daleks, Doctor Who, a large bag of marbles and a red London double decker bus. The marbles and the bus were Charlie's idea.

Charlie was just as pleased as Henry to be trying *The Newly Invented Look At The Lovely View Method* of tooth extraction. It had been explained to him very carefully by Henry, cheerful owner of four missing teeth.

Charlie was sure Henry knew what he was doing.

When Henry opened Charlie's bedroom window, he still thought so.

When Henry said, "Now lean out as far

as you can," Charlie knew it was the right thing to do.

When Henry said, "Now look at the lovely view!" Charlie looked, and he had just opened his mouth to say, "It's not that lovely," when Henry reached behind him, picked up the now enormously heavy TARDIS, said, "Trust me, I've done this millions of times," and dropped it out over the window sill.

If Max had not come in at that moment, seen what was happening and rugby tackled Charlie from right across the room, Charlie would have gone out over the window sill too.

Instead he was pinned to the window frame by Max, while from his wobbly tooth swung a TARDIS, three Daleks, Doctor Who, a bag of marbles and a London bus.

"AAAARRRRGGGHHH!" roared Charlie, and then stopped very suddenly because the TARDIS had gone smashing to the ground below, and so, attached to the piece of dental floss, had his first wobbly tooth.

"It's out!" he cried joyfully, and rushed downstairs to collect the tooth with Henry after him.

"What did you think of that?" asked Henry, bouncing with pride. "Wasn't it cool? Wasn't it great? Did you really nearly fall out of the window?"

"Yes, I did," said Charlie. "I felt my feet lift off the ground!"

"Gosh! Actually off the ground?"

"Yes. Promise. If you don't believe me, ask Max! Look at this tooth! It's got blood and everything! And it's loads bigger than I thought it would be. I'm putting it under my pillow tonight."

There were now three wobbly teeth and a dark bloody hole in Charlie's mouth, and Charlie was very happy. He and Henry showed the tooth to everyone.

"You should keep it for ever," said Max, but the grown-ups agreed that it was perfect for the tooth fairy.

Henry's mother told

Charlie something about the tooth fairy that Charlie had not known before.

"She only comes to tidy bedrooms, you know," she said.

"What?" asked Charlie, and he looked across at his own mother, who nodded in agreement, and then Henry said, "It's true. I've had to tidy mine *four times* now. Once for each tooth. And she's really fussy! It takes ages!"

"Told you the tooth fairy was a waste of time," said Max.

Charlie did not let Max put him off. He tidied his bedroom by kicking all the toys and shoes under the bed, bundling his clothes into the bottom of the wardrobe, and putting his beanbag on top of his home-made fossil-making machine.

"She's really fussy," his mum reminded

him, coming up to see how he was getting on, so Charlie stuffed the clothes in drawers, dropped the shoes over the banister into the hall, carried an armload of toys down to the living room and pushed them behind the sofa, and took the fossil-making machine to Henry's.

Now the bedroom looked much better, and Charlie was exhausted. He put his tooth under his pillow, and went to bed.

And in the night the tooth fairy came.

And she left him a brand new, solid-gold-looking, extra shiny one pound coin.

The Second Tooth

"One pound?" said Charlie. "*One pound!*
What a cheek! Henry's tooth fairy leaves
him two!"

"What?" asked Charlie's mum. "Two pounds for a tooth! She must be mad! And I don't suppose he puts it in his money box either! I bet he spends it all on sweets."

"Of course he does," said Charlie.

"Well then," said Charlie's mum, as if that was the end of the matter.

"It's not fair," Charlie complained to Henry, and Henry agreed that he was right.

"One pound!" said Charlie crossly.

"Give it to me if you don't want it," said his mother.

"Of course I want it!" said Charlie, and went with Henry to the sweet shop on the corner to spend it. They bought pickled onion rings, jelly worms, chalk lollies and bubblegum.

"Disgusting," said Charlie's mum. "Next time you have a wobbly tooth I've a good mind to leave the tooth fairy instructions saying fifty pence is plenty."

Charlie was so surprised to hear that you could leave instructions to the tooth fairy that he allowed the bubble he had just blown to burst all over his face. He thought very hard as he picked it off and chewed it up again.

"I've got an idea," he told Henry.

"What?" asked Henry, gnawing on a chalk lolly with his back teeth because he hadn't any front ones.

"I'll tell you when I get my next tooth out."

"How wobbly is your next tooth?" asked Henry, interestedly.

"Quite. Getting looser all the time."

"I am a very big expert on wobbly teeth," reminded Henry, helping himself to the last jelly worm.

"Yes, I know. Give that worm back."

"I've licked it."

"Makes no difference. Give it back."

Henry gave half back and continued, "There's *The Very Simple Remote Control Method* if you need any help."

"The what?"

"*Very Simple Remote Control Method.*"

"Does it hurt?"

"Hurt?" asked Henry. "Hurt? Why would it hurt? Do you want to try it?"

"No," said Charlie, but the next day, he said, "I might," and the day after that he said, "Perhaps," and the day after that he said, "OK."

"You have made the right decision," said Henry. "Trust me. I'm an expert."

With *The Very Simple Remote Control Method*, the end of the dental floss that was not attached to Charlie's tooth was tied to his remote controlled racing car. This was a fascinating idea to Charlie, especially (as Henry pointed out) as it had the added advantage of putting Charlie in no danger of falling out of the window.

"All done on ground level!" boasted Henry, picking up the handset. "Admit it can't go wrong!"

It went wrong because of Charlie.

Charlie simply could not bear to stand still while the car drove away with his tooth.

"Don't run after it!" shrieked Henry, nearly dead with laughing, but Charlie could not help running after it.

The faster Henry raced the car round and round the garden, the faster Charlie ran. For a while Henry had a remote control friend, and he made Charlie race forward, and skid round corners and do handbrake turns and sudden changes of direction, all the time with his mouth wide open and roaring, "NOOOOOOOOOO!!!!"

It was the most fun Henry had had for ages. He would have kept it up all afternoon if Charlie had not fallen down on top of the car.

Charlie's racing car lost a wheel, Charlie himself hurt both his knees, and when he attacked Henry to try and stop him laughing, the aerial on the handset was broken off. It was not until Henry was flat on his stomach with Charlie on top of him stuffing grass down the back of his neck, that Charlie suddenly realized that his mouth felt different.

"My tooth!" he exclaimed, and there it was, jagged and wonderful and still tied to the car.

"My remote control tooth!" said Charlie, dribbling blood as he gloated over it.

"You might say 'thank you'," remarked Henry, picking sticks and grass out from the neck of his shirt. "It would still be stuck in your mouth if it wasn't for me."

"Oh, well, thank you, I suppose," said

Charlie. "You might say 'sorry' for making me break my car."

"If you like," agreed Henry. "Sorry, then. But I expect Max will be able to mend it."

"Not the aerial," said Charlie. "We've broken them before. They don't mend; you have to buy new ones. They cost about a million pounds!"

"A million pounds!" repeated Henry, scornfully. "They don't!"

"Yes, they do. If you don't believe me, ask Max!"

"I will," said Henry, and went with Charlie when he took the car inside.

Charlie showed Max the new bloody hole in his mouth beside the old bloody hole in his mouth, his two remaining wobbly teeth, and the broken car.

Max admired the holes, wobbled the

teeth, and looked
carefully at
the car. The
wheel could
be mended
no problem,
he said, but the
handset would need
a new aerial, which would
cost about a million pounds.

"Still, it got my tooth out!" said Charlie,
cheerfully.

Max pointed out that since Charlie
would only get a pound for his tooth
(and only fifty pence if the tooth fairy
followed their mum's instructions) this
proved once again that all this tooth
fairy nonsense was a complete waste of
time.

"Forget the tooth fairy!" Max advised Charlie.

"No!" said Charlie. "I've got an idea for a very good plan."

That night Charlie did not leave his tooth under his pillow. He left a carefully written set of instructions.

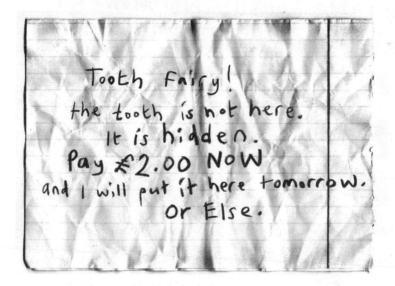

Tooth Fairy!
the tooth is not here.
It is hidden.
Pay £2.00 NOW
and I will put it here tomorrow.
or Else.

But it seemed that the tooth fairy was tough, or perhaps she didn't like being bossed about. Charlie's note was still there in the morning, but now there was a message on the back.

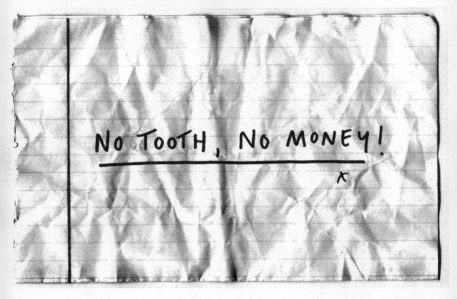

The Third Tooth

"No tooth, no money!" said Charlie,
furiously. "What kind of a fairy is that?
What'll I do now?"

"Keep your teeth," said Max. "Like I told
you before."

"What were you thinking of?" asked his
mother. "Two pounds for a tooth! Not in
this house!"

"It's two pounds for a tooth in Henry's house," said Charlie, sulkily. "And anyway, she could have left me one pound at least! She could have left me something!"

"You didn't leave her anything," pointed out his mother. "And you didn't tidy either! Anyway, never mind, you can always put your tooth under your pillow and try again. You'll just have to wait till tomorrow."

"But I don't want to wait till tomorrow," protested Charlie.

"Well, if you really don't want to wait till tomorrow," said his mother, "you could pretend I am a tooth fairy! I will give you fifty pence to do what you like with for that tooth, and a nice crunchy apple besides."

"Fifty pence?" asked Charlie, looking at the tooth in his hand. "Is that all?"

"Yes," said his mother. "And a nice

crunchy apple, sliced up because you haven't any bottom teeth. And a piece of flapjack just out of the oven if you wait five minutes for it to cool a bit."

"I bet you give Max a piece of flapjack too," said Charlie bitterly.

"I probably will," agreed his mother. "Since he has just taken the rubbish out, and vacuumed the hall and brushed down the stairs."

Charlie sighed, and looked at the flapjack.

"What about Henry?" he asked. "We always share."

"Oh, all right," said his mother. "Here's my final offer. Fifty pence to do what you like with. One crunchy apple sliced up because you haven't any bottom teeth. Two pieces of flapjack, one for Henry."

"I'll take the money and the flapjack," said Charlie, at last. "Forget the apple."

"The apple was part of the deal," said the pretend tooth fairy sternly.

Charlie and Henry had a feast at Henry's house. First the apple to get rid of it. Then the flapjack. Then the long red liquorice bootlaces that they had bought with Charlie's fifty pence, and which they made last all afternoon by sucking them like spaghetti in and out of the gaps in their teeth until Henry's mother ordered them to chew them up before she went mad.

And then everything was eaten, and
Charlie said, "What'll we do now?"

"How are your other wobbly teeth?"
asked Henry.

Charlie tested them. They were both
much wobblier than they had been earlier
in the day, particularly one that had got
itself stuck in a bite of flapjack.

"You've got quite a bit of movement
there," said Henry, looking at it with

interest. "Keep pushing. I've got a good idea about that tooth."

"So have I," said Charlie, "I'm going to put it under *your* pillow!"

"*Under my pillow?*"

"Yes, and then I'll get two pounds instead of one."

"Would that work?" wondered Henry, and he ran downstairs with Charlie after him, and asked his mother, "Mum, would it work if Charlie put his tooth under my pillow instead of his own?"

"I expect so," said Henry's mother. "But why on earth would he want to do that?"

"So as to get two pounds instead of one," explained Charlie.

"Good grief!" said Henry's mother, looking very startled indeed. "Are you telling me the tooth fairy gets away with

paying just one pound
at your house,
Charlie?"

Charlie nodded.

"It can't be
the same fairy,"
said Henry's
mother, and then
she added, rather
hopefully, "Of course,

there is no telling which fairy will come
here next time. It might easily never be the
two pound one again. . ."

"It might be the ten pound note one,"
said Henry, glaring at his mother through
half closed eyes. "Have you thought of
that?"

"No, no, no," said his mother, hastily.
"There's no such thing as a ten pound

note fairy! Don't be silly, Henry! And don't forget to warn Charlie that the tooth fairy who visits this house only comes for absolutely sparkling clean and tidy bedrooms. So you might want to think again about leaving your next tooth here, Charlie!"

"Oh no," said Charlie, cheerfully. "I'm dead quick at tidying up."

"She checks under the bed," warned Henry's mother. "And inside the wardrobe for things in heaps at the bottom. And all the toys have to be sorted into the right boxes and stacked very neatly. And that's before you even start on the vacuuming. . ."

"Vacuuming?"

"And dusting. . ."

"Dusting?"

"Pairing up socks. . ."

"What?"

"Bringing down shoes, and recycling and rubbish! Organizing the bookcase! And (of course) cleaning out that dreadful smelly hamster!"

"He doesn't smell at all!" said Henry, indignantly. "Only of hamster! Who could mind the lovely smell of hamster? Come on, Charlie! Let's go and do things at your house! Your tooth isn't even out yet!"

"I know, but I think you should tidy up your room ready for when it is."

"I should tidy it?" asked Henry. "It's your tooth!"

"It's your mess!"

"It's not just mine!" said Henry. "It's at least half yours! The den was your idea, and all those tins of mud you stuffed under my bed yesterday."

"They are not tins of mud," said Charlie. "They are Science. They are a fossil-making machine. That's how fossils are *made*, with mud! If you don't believe me, ask Max. Anyway, if I help you tidy, will you let my tooth go under your pillow?"

"Oh, all right," agreed Henry.

"It's definitely loosening," said Charlie, waggling it with a finger as hard as he could bear. "Do you know any more good ways of getting teeth out quickly?"

"I might be able to remember one," said Henry cautiously. "If you let me lie down

and think. If you like, *I'll* go to your house
and lie down and think in *your* bedroom,
while *you* begin tidying in mine."

"Do you think I'm bonkers?" demanded
Charlie. "We'll *both* lie down and think, and
then we'll *both* tidy!"

They started the thinking straight away,
lying side by side amongst the fossil-making
machine on Henry's carpet.

Henry finished his thinking first. It was easier for him to think of ways of getting rid of teeth quickly because it was not his tooth that was going to be got rid of. Whenever Charlie had a good tooth-pulling idea it always ended with the worrying question, "But wouldn't that hurt?" Henry did not have any problems like that, which was how he thought of *The Spectacular Flying Arrow Extraction System*, the same as Robin Hood probably used.

At first Henry kept his idea a secret because if it worked (and he was sure it would) he would have to tidy his bedroom. But it was a hard secret to keep with Charlie beside him muttering, "What about. . . Oh yes! Only wouldn't that hurt?" and jiggling his tooth as he thought, so that it got looser and looser all the time.

It would be a shame, thought Henry, if Charlie's tooth fell out by itself, before he had time to try out his idea. And so he said to Charlie, "There *is* one very good way. . ."

At first Charlie said, "No."

"But you want your tooth out!"

"Not like that. It would definitely hurt! I know it would."

"How can you know till you've tried it?" asked Henry.

"I can guess!"

"Charlie," said Henry, in a very quiet kind voice, like a dentist. "I promise you won't feel a thing. (Hardly.) It's the way everyone did it in the olden days, before they had upstairs windows and remote control cars."

"I'll just wobble it," said Charlie, and for the next two days that was what he did.

And for the next two days, Henry said, "Oh, come on, let me do it! There's nothing on telly! I'm so bored!"

"Don't let Henry pull your teeth out just because there's nothing on telly!" Max told Charlie.

"I won't," said Charlie.

So the third wobbly tooth stayed where it was.

It was loose. It was so loose Charlie could stick it out between his two closed lips, like a fang.

But it didn't come out.

And there was nothing on telly.

And Charlie was bored too.

So at last he said, "OK, Henry. Fetch the dental floss!"

With *The Spectacular Flying Arrow Extraction System*, the end of the thread that was not fastened to Charlie's tooth was tied to an arrow from Charlie's bow and arrow set.

Then Charlie and Henry went into the garden and Henry said, "Now give me the bow."

"No," said Charlie. "Not this time! I gave you the remote control handset and look what happened!"

Charlie fitted the arrow to the bowstring himself.

And then he pulled back the string as far

as it would go.

And he stood like that for quite a long time, until Henry suddenly shouted, "Fire!" and Charlie, who was not expecting him to do this, jumped in surprise.

The arrow flew into the air, and
Charlie's tooth went with it. Higher and
higher they soared, in a wonderful curve
with nothing but blue sky behind.
And they landed perfectly
safely at the end of
the garden.

And after that the only thing left to do
was tidy Henry's bedroom.

Which took ages.

The Fourth Tooth

The next day Charlie called for Henry at half past five in the morning.

"Goodness, Charlie," groaned Henry's mum, blinking and yawning on the doorstep. "Did you have to ring the bell *and* hammer quite so hard? I'm sure. . ."

But Charlie had already hurried past her into the house, raced up the stairs to Henry's bedroom, shoved his sleeping friend out of the way, and snatched aside his pillow.

"Go awayyyyy!" groaned Henry, as his head hit the mattress. "Gerroff my bed! Give me back my pillow!"

"Got it!" rejoiced Charlie, grabbing an envelope from beside Henry's ear.

"Good. Go home then," said Henry.

Charlie did not go home. He bounced down on to the bed, ripped open the envelope, and tipped into his hand two lovely round pound coins.

Then Charlie got very noisy indeed,

jumping round the bedroom, shouting, "Ha!
Brilliant! Amazing!" and singing, "I tricked
the tooth fairy! I tricked the tooth fairy!"
and shaking Henry and demanding that he
wake up properly, and look.

Henry groaned, rubbed his eyes, looked
and remarked, "You ought to give one of
them to me!"

"I'm not!" said Charlie.

"That's mean then! It was my idea that
got the tooth out! And my pillow that you
put it under. In my bedroom that I had to
help tidy. It was MY tooth fairy!"

"It was MY tooth!" said Charlie.

"Show-off!"

"Grabber!"

"Greedy pig!"

"Like your pyjamas!" jeered Charlie,
which was particularly unkind because they

were the Thomas the Tank Engine ones
that Henry vowed he never wore.

So then Henry got on top
of Charlie with his beanbag
and squashed him flat.

Charlie went all silent
and limp to frighten
him.

"You've
not fainted or
something, have
you?" asked
Henry, lifting off the
beanbag, and Charlie lunged out, got him
round the knees, rolled him up in his quilt
and pushed him under his bed.

Henry sat up under his bed, burst
through the wooden slats that made the
base, and heaved the mattress at his friend.

The bookcase fell over and so did the hamster cage. The fossil-making machine was wrecked. Henry's mother came in and said in a dreadful voice, "STOP!"

Charlie and Henry tidied Henry's bedroom in absolute silence while Henry's mother stood in the doorway and glared. When it was done she said, "Henry, you are grounded. Charlie, go home."

Charlie had been sent home in disgrace from Henry's house many times before, probably almost as many as Henry had been sent home from Charlie's house. So he went away quite cheerfully. He was feeling very pleased with himself. He had successfully tricked the tooth fairy with his third wobbly tooth. He had seen Henry wearing Thomas the Tank Engine pyjamas with his own eyes. And he had two pounds to do what he liked with.

That afternoon Charlie spent the whole
two pounds on a giant bag of butterscotch
popcorn that he took out into the street
to show Henry, who was staring gloomily
through his bedroom window, still grounded.

Charlie mimed gobbling the popcorn all
up.

Henry mimed jumping out of the window
and killing him.

Charlie mimed that he would save the
last crumb for
Henry.

Henry turned
down his mouth
and shrugged his
shoulders to show
that he couldn't
care less.

Then Charlie swaggered on down the street, but when he turned back to wave before going into his own house he caught sight of Henry's face.

Henry was not miming. He just looked sad.

So Charlie went inside feeling awful and the first thing he did was go and hunt for Max. And not long afterwards he came out of his house again, and ran back down the street to Henry's front door.

Charlie knocked on Henry's door with his best respectful knocking, and when Henry's mother opened it he said in his politest voice, "Please, I am very sorry I woke you up so early in the morning and wrecked Henry's bedroom and fought him (he started it, though) and please may I go up and be grounded with him too? Because

that is only fair, Max said. And I really am
sorry, not just saying it. I promise. If you
don't believe me, ask Max."

"All right, Charlie," said Henry's
mother, at last.

It was brilliant being grounded with
Henry. They turned Henry's bedroom

into a cinema by drawing the curtains and watched telly all afternoon with the bag of popcorn between them.

At first they talked about what they would buy when Charlie's fourth wobbly tooth fell out, and how important it was to keep the bedroom tidy so as to be able to trick the tooth fairy again. And they talked about popcorn, and how much they liked the hard crunchy bits that were solid butterscotch, and how Charlie always sucked them, and how Henry always munched them up quick.

But soon they stopped talking. They were sleepy from being up so early. They chomped and watched telly and chomped and dreamed and forgot about teeth. Popcorn got spilled and was eaten off the floor. Charlie was half asleep when Henry suddenly remembered an idea he had had while he was busy being grounded and said, "So what about making a tooth fairy trap?"

Charlie was so suprised that a handful of popcorn went down the wrong way and he choked and coughed it all over the floor. And in the fuss of picking it up again the whole bag was knocked over.

ACK

From downstairs Henry's mum, who seemed to have developed the power to see through ceilings, called warningly, "Henry! Charlie!"

"Pick it up," whispered Henry urgently, "before she comes up and goes mad again. She's been awful all day."

They scrabbled about on their hands and knees in the dim cinema light, collecting popcorn and tidying it into their mouths as they found it.

"Isn't it strange," remarked Henry, crunching a particularly hard piece of butterscotch, "how the top bit of the bag tastes fantastic, and the middle bit is OK but boring, and the last bit is just nasty but you can't seem to stop . . . CHARLIE! Your tooth!"

"What?"

"Put the light on! Put the light on!" squeaked Henry, and raced and put it on himself.

But all at once Charlie did not need light to know what had happened.

It had gone. His fourth and last wobbly tooth. Vanished, all by itself, with no help from anyone.

"*Where* has it gone?" moaned Henry, because the switching on of the light had revealed something even more shocking. Amongst the spilled and scattered popcorn all over the floor there were pieces that were stained with. . .

"Blood!" howled Henry. "No wonder it didn't taste right!"

"Oh, what does it matter what it tasted like?" wailed Charlie. "Help me find my tooth!"

But the tooth could not be found.

Charlie and Henry searched and

searched. So did Max, when they fetched him to help them. They looked under everything, and on top of everything, and between everything. They picked up every fragment of popcorn, and every piece they picked up looked like a tooth.

They carried on searching until there was no doubt left at all.

And then Max made the awful announcement.

"One of you," said Max, "must have eaten it."

"*Eaten my tooth?*" asked Charlie.

"By mistake," said Max.

"But you'd know!" said Charlie. "It would be hard! It would crunch!"

Henry groaned. He knew who had eaten Charlie's tooth. He had guessed it ages ago. He could even feel it, like a tooth-shaped

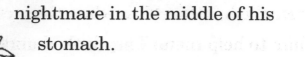

nightmare in the middle of his stomach.

In the kitchen, the mothers were drinking coffee and complaining about the amount of sweets Charlie and Henry ate (which they thought were far too many) and the school holidays (which they thought were far too long) when the boys burst in.

"What does the tooth fairy do," demanded Charlie, "if the tooth gets eaten?"

"What?" exclaimed the mothers. "Who's eaten a tooth?"

"Henry has!"

"I didn't even know he had wobbly

ones," said Henry's mother, very surprised.

"He doesn't. It was mine," said Charlie, showing them his latest gory gap.

"Henry ate your tooth?" asked Charlie's mother.

"He crunched it up. He thought it was popcorn. . . Oh, stop laughing! It isn't funny! What I need to know is, does the tooth fairy *have to have the actual tooth*?"

"Yes!" said both mothers instantly.

Teeth

Charlie said it wasn't fair.

"Just because she's called a fairy doesn't mean she's fair," said his mother.

"Besides," said Henry's mother, "you and Henry have had enough sweets lately to last you for months."

"There must be something we can do," said Charlie. "What about if we

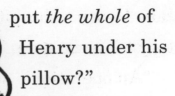

put *the whole* of Henry under his pillow?"

The mothers shook their heads.

"*Tidily* under his pillow?" asked Charlie, remembering the extreme fussiness of the tooth fairy.

"No," said the mothers cheerfully. "Wouldn't work."

"Why not?"

"Because there wouldn't be a tooth, would there?" explained Henry's mother. "Not an actual tooth that anyone could take away."

"No tooth, no money!" Charlie's mother reminded him.

"Well," said Charlie, desperately, "let's

take Henry to hospital to have an operation to get it back again."

"An operation!" squealed Henry. "What sort of operation?"

"A getting-my-tooth-back-operation!"

"How?"

"Well, I suppose they'd slice you open or something," said Charlie sulkily.

"No!" yelled Henry, and the mothers explained that doctors and surgeons were far too busy to slice people open for the sake of a swallowed tooth, no matter who it belonged to.

"I *hate* the tooth fairy!" growled Charlie.

"So do I!" said Henry.

"Come with me," said Max.

Max and Charlie shared a bedroom, but

that did not mean that they did not each have their own private places. Charlie, for instance, had an old brown bear that was practically hollow. Max had. . .

Charlie didn't know what Max had. Max was clever. Max's secrets were hidden.

But now Max led Charlie and Henry to a battered grey box in the corner of the bedroom labelled: HOMEWORK SHEETS.

From the homework sheets box Max took a pair of football socks, unwashed and rolled into a ball.

From the middle of the ball of football socks he unwrapped a very small book which he handed to Charlie.

COLLINS ENGLISH DICTIONARY, it said on the cover.

"So what?" asked Charlie, and Max laughed.

Charlie and Henry looked at each other, completely puzzled, because who could be pleased to be shown a dictionary, especially a dictionary that came out of a ball of dirty socks? Socks from a box labelled HOMEWORK SHEETS.

"Open it," said Max.

It was not a book, it was a book made

into a box. The pages had been glued together, and a rough rectangular hollow cut in the middle of them, so that when the front cover was lifted a secret space was revealed.

In that secret space were teeth.

Max shook them and they rattled like strange small stones, cream coloured, faintly gleaming. A weird, eerie collection of chisel-edged front teeth and back ones like a miniature range of ancient hills.

"Twelve so far," said Max, and then he wrapped them carefully up again, put them in his pocket and went away.

Charlie and Henry had seen some cool things in their lives.

Their friend Sam had a fake stick-on wound that made anywhere he stuck it look sliced wide open.

At a Halloween party they had been given blood-red jelly with plastic glow in the dark fingernails sprinkled on the top.

In Science they had seen a model of a person whose skin lifted off in sections to show his life-size multicoloured bulging insides.

They had thought those things were cool.

But in all their lives they had never seen anything as cool as Max's secret collection of teeth.

They were not models, or plastic, or fake from the joke shop.

They were real.

"I wish I'd kept my teeth!" said Charlie sadly.

"Yes, think what you could do," agreed Henry, "if you had a whole lot like that?"

"You could make a fantastic cannibal necklace."

"You could make a horror mask with plasticine lips and real teeth."

"Imagine freezing them. Trick ice cubes for parties!"

"Or you could just keep them for ever," said Henry. "In a hollowed out book, like Max's. That book was amazing!"

"Let's make one each," said Charlie.

"Yes," said Henry, eagerly. "And fill them with teeth! Our teeth! Who'll have the next wobbly one?"

"If you do," said Charlie, "I can help you get it out! I've nearly finished inventing *The Washing Line Zip Wire Easy Out Experience!*"

"If you do," said Henry, "there's *The Tasty Toffee Tooth Tugger* that we haven't tried yet!"

"But what about the tooth fairy?" asked Charlie and Henry's mothers when they heard the latest news.

"If we get rid of the tooth fairy we'll never have to tidy our bedrooms again!" said Henry.

"The tooth fairy," said Charlie, "is for kids!"

"What kind of person," asked Henry scornfully, "sells their own teeth?"

"And who wants fairies crawling round their beds when they're asleep?" added Charlie.

"Not me!" said Henry.

"The tooth fairy," said Charlie, "is a waste of teeth. And if you don't believe us, ask Max!"

"Look out for more of my adventures!"

Meet Charlie – he's trouble!

Charlie and Henry are staying the night at Charlie's house. They've made a deal, but the night doesn't go quite as Charlie plans. . .

Charlie's fed up with his mean family always picking on him – so he's decided to run away.
That'll show them! Now they'll be sorry!
But running away means being boringly, IMPOSSIBLY quiet…

Meet Charlie – he's trouble!

"The snow's all getting wasted! What'll we do? It will never last till after school!"

Charlie's been waiting for snow his whole life, but now it's come, everyone's trying to spoil it! Luckily, Charlie has a very clever plan to keep it safe…

"Zachary is a liar, liar, pants on fire!"

There's a new boy in Charlie's class. Zachary says his dad is away on a rocket but Charlie knows that's rubbish … Isn't it?

Meet Charlie – he's trouble!

Charlie has given up cheese and onion crisps!

He just hasn't been himself lately. There's only one thing for it - the Truly Amazing Smarties Trick!

Charlie's big brother Max isn't scared of anything ... Except Aunt Emma's spooky house.

At last it's Charlie's chance to be the hero. Those ghosts had better watch out!